Essex County Counci
D0184659

Hansel and Gretel

by Lynne Benton and Louise Forshaw

Hansel and Gretel lived with their father and stepmother in a small cottage by the forest. Their father worked hard, but the family were poor.

One day, their stepmother said, “Go to the forest. We need wood for the fire. Here, take your breakfast with you.”

The children were scared of
the big, dark forest.
"We'll get lost," said Gretel.
"No, we won't," said Hansel.
"We can leave a trail of breadcrumbs.
We can follow the trail home later."

They collected lots of wood for
the fire. When it was time to go home,
they looked for the trail of breadcrumbs.
But the birds had eaten them.

The children kept walking,

and soon they came to a cottage.

“Look,” cried Gretel.

“It’s made of sweets.”

"I'm so hungry!" said Hansel.

He broke off a sweet and ate it.

The door of the cottage opened,
and an old woman came out.
She looked kind.
"Come in, children," she said.
"I have lots more sweets inside."

Hansel and Gretel went into the cottage.

The old woman grabbed Hansel. She pushed him inside a cage and locked the door. Then the old woman looked at Gretel.

She didn't look kind any more.

She looked like ... a witch!

"When he gets fat, I will eat him," she cackled. "And now you will work for me!"

Gretel worked hard every day, scrubbing the floor and polishing the witch's gold coins.
The witch gave Hansel lots of food to make him fat. But she gave Gretel just scraps of food.

The witch could not see very well.

Every day, she made Hansel put out

his finger to feel if he was getting fat.

But clever Hansel held out

a chicken bone instead.

"Still too thin!" grumbled the witch.

One day, the witch snapped,
"I'm not waiting any longer.
Today, I will eat you anyway!"
She lit the oven. After a while,
she told Gretel to get inside
and see if it was hot enough.

But clever Gretel said, “I’m too big.

I won’t fit inside.”

“Don’t be silly!” cried the witch.

“I will show you. Even I can fit inside!”

And she opened the oven door.

Quickly, Gretel pushed the witch into the oven and slammed the door. Then she opened the cage and let Hansel out.

“Let’s go home,” she said.

“We’ll take the gold coins with us.”

The birds flew ahead to lead the way.

Their father was so happy to see them.
"Look what we've got, Father!"
cried Gretel. Hansel gave him the gold.
"Gold is good, but having you home
is better!" their father said.

Story order

Look at these 5 pictures and captions.
Put the pictures in the right order
to retell the story.

1

Gretel pushed the witch into the oven.

2

Their father was pleased to have
them home again.

3

The children found a cottage.

4

The birds ate the breadcrumbs.

5

The witch locked Hansel in a cage.

Guide for Independent Reading

This series is designed to provide an opportunity for your child to read on their own. These notes are written for you to help your child choose a book and to read it independently.
In school, your child's teacher will often be using reading books which have been banded to support the process of learning to read. Use the book band colour your child is reading in school to help you make a good choice. *Hansel and Gretel* is a good choice for children reading at Turquoise Band in their classroom to read independently.
The aim of independent reading is to read this book with ease, so that your child enjoys the story and relates it to their own experiences.

About the book

When Hansel and Gretel get lost in the forest, they find an amazing cottage made of sweets. But the old lady who lives there is not as kind as she first seems.

Before reading

Help your child to learn how to make good choices by asking:
"Why did you choose this book? Why do you think you will enjoy it?"
Look at the cover together and ask: "What do you think the story will be about?" Ask your child to think of what they already know about the story context. Then ask your child to read the title aloud.
Ask: "Where do you think Hansel and Gretel are? How do you think they are feeling?"
Remind your child that they can sound out a word in syllable chunks if they get stuck.
Decide together whether your child will read the story independently or read it aloud to you.

During reading

Remind your child of what they know and what they can do independently. If reading aloud, support your child if they hesitate or ask for help by telling the word. If reading to themselves, remind your child that they can come and ask for your help if stuck.

After reading

Support comprehension by asking your child to tell you about the story. Use the story order puzzle to encourage your child to retell the story in the right sequence, in their own words. The correct sequence can be found on the next page.

Help your child think about the messages in the book that go beyond the story and ask: "What do you think Hansel and Gretel should have done differently?" Give your child a chance to respond to the story: "Did you have a favourite part? If you could have a house made of your favourite things, what would it be made of?"

Extending learning

Help your child understand the story structure by using the same sentence patterning and adding different elements. "Let's make up a new story about Hansel and Gretel. Where might they get lost this time and what might they find?"

In the classroom, your child's teacher may be teaching use of punctuation marks. Ask your child to identify some question marks and exclamation marks in the story and then ask them to practise reading each of the whole sentences with appropriate expression.

Franklin Watts
First published in Great Britain in 2021
by The Watts Publishing Group

Series Editors: Jackie Hamley and Melanie Palmer
Series Advisors: Dr Sue Bodman and Glen Franklin
Series Designers: Peter Scoulding and Cathryn Gilbert

A CIP catalogue record for this book is
available from the British Library.

ISBN 978 1 4451 7706 9 (hbk)
ISBN 978 1 4451 7707 6 (pbk)
ISBN 978 1 4451 7705 2 (library ebook)
ISBN 978 1 4451 8149 3 (ebook)

Printed in China

Franklin Watts
An imprint of
Hachette Children's Group
Part of The Watts Publishing Group
Carmelite House
50 Victoria Embankment
London EC4Y 0DZ

An Hachette UK Company
www.hachette.co.uk

www.franklinwatts.co.uk

Answer to Story order: 4, 3, 5, 1, 2